Text copyright © 2015 by Louise Borden.
Illustrations copyright © 2015 by Genevieve Godbout.
All rights reserved. No part of this book
may be reproduced in any form without
written permission from the publisher.

Library of Congress Cataloging-in-Publication Data:
Borden, Louise, author.
Kindergarten luck / by Louise Borden ; illustrations by
Genevieve Godbout.
pages cm
Summary: After he finds a brand new shiny penny,
Theodore has a perfect day in Kindergarten.
ISBN 978-1-4521-1394-4 (alk. paper)
1. Kindergarten—Juvenile fiction. 2. Fortune—Juvenile
fiction. 3. Coins—Juvenile fiction. [1. Kindergarten—
Fiction. 2. Schools—Fiction. 3. Luck—Fiction. 4. Coins—
Fiction.] I. Godbout, Genevieve, illustrator. II. Title.

PZ7.B64827Ki 2015
813.54—dc23
2014001513

Manufactured in China.

FSC
www.fsc.org
MIX
Paper from
responsible sources
FSC® C104723

Design by Amelia Mack.
Typeset in Revers and KG Cold Coffee.
The illustrations in this book were rendered in
colored pencil.

10 9 8 7 6 5 4 3 2 1

Chronicle Books LLC
680 Second Street
San Francisco, California 94107

www.chroniclekids.com

Kindergarten Luck

By **Louise Borden** · Illustrated by **Genevieve Godbout**

chronicle books · san francisco

One gloomy morning,
Theodore found a bright, shiny penny
on the way down to breakfast.
There was Abraham Lincoln, face up.

What
luck!

"Oh, thank you,
mr. Famous
President!"

Theodore said.

And he tucked that shiny,
new penny in his pocket.

"You make the best pancakes,"

Theodore told Mama
when she kissed him good-bye.

The gloomy rain
suddenly **stopped**
and the September sun
came out.

Theodore and Louisa
raced each other to the bus stop
on Cherry Street.

Number 19 was on time, and so were they!

There was Slim,
Theodore's favorite bus driver,
with his morning news:

"I heard a rumor that next week

the zoo is bringing real penguins to school."

Hooray! Hooray!

Number 19 got really noisy until Slim hushed everyone.

Then the bus pulled up at Riverside School, the **best** school in the **whole world** as Theodore was always telling his friend Georgia.

He counted the puffy white clouds floating right over the yellow line of buses;

the sky was **blue**
such a **lucky blue!**

Theodore and Georgia
swung their backpacks and waved to
other kids who were in their class.

Right away,

Mr. Leland called on Theodore to show the class
the day of the week and the date
on the big wall calendar.

And later,
during Writing Time,
Mr. Leland read **Theodore's**
poem out loud.

Lucky Little Clouds
High in the sky...
floating by floating by

At recess, Theodore swatted the tetherball

again

and again

and again

and again

and again

without missing **once.**

His friends all cheered for him
while Georgia ran off
to tell Mr. Leland.

Then the end-of-recess whistle blew,
and everyone lined up to go inside.
Theodore was chosen to be the line leader.

And all the time,
he was carrying that penny,
that shiny, lucky penny in his pocket.

He took a quick peek at Abraham Lincoln . . . and whispered,

"Thank you,
Mr. Famous President."

After Science, the class walked up the hall to the media center (Mr. Leland said to be as quiet as kindergarten mice), and Theodore got to type **his own words** on a brand-new computer and check out a giant book about **penguins.**

Penguins have wings that are shaped like paddles...

Then Mr. Leland
picked Vijay
and Abigail
and Eduardo
and Leia
and **Theodore**
to help Miss Walker, the art teacher,
hang the kindergarten's Matisse pictures
in the school lobby.

Ms. Agresta, the principal, strolled out
of the Office and said the paintings were "so jazzy"
that she was going to show them off at the Riverside Family Night the next week.

Then Mrs. Cooper, the school secretary, announced on the loudspeaker that students in Grade 3 were to meet in the gym to practice their special welcome song for Family Night.

On the way back to his kindergarten room,
Theodore walked as **slowly** as a turtle,
so he could wave to Louisa . . .
because **she** was a third grader.

(That's why Theodore knew
the words to the special song, too,
and could hum along.)

Later in Math, when Mr. Leland showed the class how to add numbers, Theodore reached in his left pocket just to check on . . .

OH, GOSH!

And he gulped a big gulp.

Where was his . . .

Then Theodore remembered he'd put the penny in his **right** pocket.

When Mr. Leland asked the class how many puppies were in a litter of 1 puppy plus 6 puppies,

Theodore raised his hand And said, "Seven!"

The Riverside buzzer rang at 3:25 p.m., and there was Theodore's bus, good old Number 19, revving its engine, ready to take students home.

Theodore couldn't wait to tell Slim about the wonderful things that had happened to him. He sat in the row behind Slim's driver seat . . .

and he showed Slim his penguin book,

and they talked about the luck in the world,

and how sometimes,

it's just waiting for you
to find it.

When Number 19 rumbled up Cherry Street
and Slim put on the brakes,
Theodore took his Lincoln penny
out of his pocket
       (his **right** pocket)
and held it for a minute, **thinking.**

Then, quiet as a kindergarten mouse,
Theodore slid his penny
face up on the floor
next to Slim's seat.

Louisa and Theodore got off at the corner
and waved good-bye.

The September sun was still shining.

The sky was still blue.

And there were still little white clouds to watch.

The day hadn't been gloomy after all.

Theodore had found

his own luck in a shiny penny . . .

enough to give to a friend

. . . and enough for tomorrow, too.